OLIVER JEFFE...

An
ALPHABET
of STORIES

A B C D E F
G H I J K L
M N O P Q R
S T U V W
X Y Z

HarperCollins Children's Books

To Dad

Thanks for never making
us get a real job.

Love Oliver and Rory

First published in hardback in Great Britain
as *Once Upon an Alphabet* in 2014
This edition published in 2018

10 9 8 7 6 5 4 3 2 1

ISBN: 978-0-00-751429-8

Design by Rory Jeffers

HarperCollins Children's Books is a division
of HarperCollins Publishers Ltd.

Text and illustrations copyright © Oliver Jeffers 2014, 2018

Visit our website at www.harpercollins.co.uk

Printed in China

Aa

An ASTRONAUT

Edmund was an astronaut.

For ages he'd been training
to go on an adventure up into
space to meet some aliens.

Although there was a problem.

Space was about three hundred and twenty-eight
thousand, four hundred and sixteen feet above him...

...and Edmund had a fear of heights.

Anything over three feet in the air was a
bit much for him. He had a long way to go.

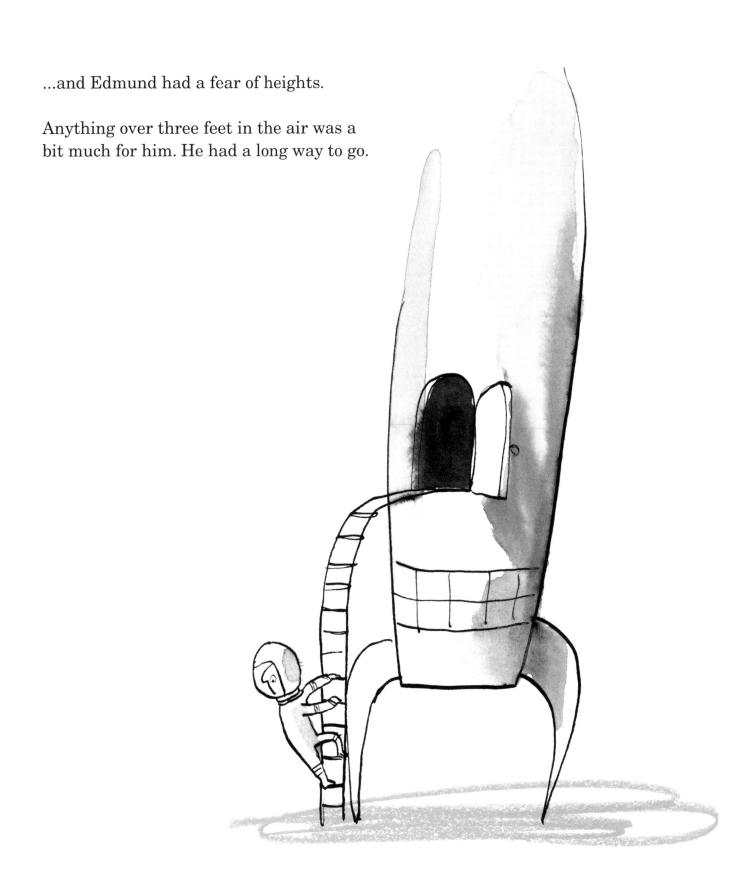

Another three hundred and twenty-eight
thousand, four hundred and thirteen feet
to be accurate.

B b

BURNING A BRIDGE

Bernard and Bob lived on either side of a bridge and for years had been battling each other for reasons neither could remember.

One day Bob decided to fix things so Bernard couldn't bother him anymore, by burning the bridge between them.

But Bob learned an important lesson that day.

He needed the bridge to get back.

cup in the
cupboard

Cup lived in the cupboard. It was dark
and cold in there when the door was closed.

He dreamed of living over by the window
where he'd have a clear view.

One afternoon, he decided to go for it.

Unfortunately, he forgot that
the counter was a long way
down, and made of concrete.

DANGER DELILAH

Danger Delilah is a daredevil
who laughs in the face of Death
and dances at the door of Disaster.

Nothing is too dangerous
and she fears no one...

* DON'T TRY this at HOME

...except her dad when she's late for dinner.

Ee

An
ENIGMA

How many elephants can
you fit inside an envelope?

Turn to the letter N to find out...

Forever

Ferdinand was out walking his frog,
when he came upon a hole. A really big hole.

In fact it was the world's biggest hole and
it went on forever.

He dropped a penny in to see how long it
would take to hit the bottom.

Would you believe me if
I told you it's still falling?

That's because
forever never ends...

GUARDing THINGS

Leopold Picard is a really great guard.

He'll guard anything he is given,
provided he is asked nicely enough.
(Good manners are very important you know.)

His current assignment is a bit
boring. But he doesn't mind.

It's much better than his last one.

Half a
HOUSE

Helen lived in half a house.
The other half had fallen into the sea
during a hurricane a year and a half ago.

Being lazy, and not owning a hammer,
she hadn't quite got around to fixing it yet.
Which was fine…

...until the horrible day she
rolled out the wrong side of bed.

The INVENTOR

There once lived an ingenious inventor
who invented many ingenious things.

His latest invention allowed him to
observe iguanas in their natural habitat...

...incognito.

Jj

JELLY DOOR

You can do all sorts of things with jelly.

You can eat it. You can throw it.
You can make stuff out of it.

That's what Jemima did. She made
her front door out of jelly. That way,
if she ever left home without her keys,
she could just reach in and grab them.

Of course, so could anyone else.

Because of that, the jelly door
never did catch on.

But, sure, who would be so
foolish as to forget their keys
in the first place?

K k

The KING

The King of France
Went out for a dance
And forgot to bring along keys.

He got locked out
And sat about
All night with no sleep
And no cheese.

The LUMBERJACK's Light

Jack Stack the Lumberjack has been struck by lightning one hundred and eleven times in his life so far. What lousy luck, you might think.

Well, the first few times were annoying, but he is actually beginning to like it now.

For one thing, he is so live with electricity...

...that he no longer needs
a plug for his light at night.

MADE of MATTER

Mary is made of matter.
So is her mother.
And her mother's moose.

In fact, matter makes up
everything from magnets
and maps to mountains
and mattresses.

Mary discovered all of
this the marvellous day
she got sucked through
a microscope and became
the size of a molecule. ✗

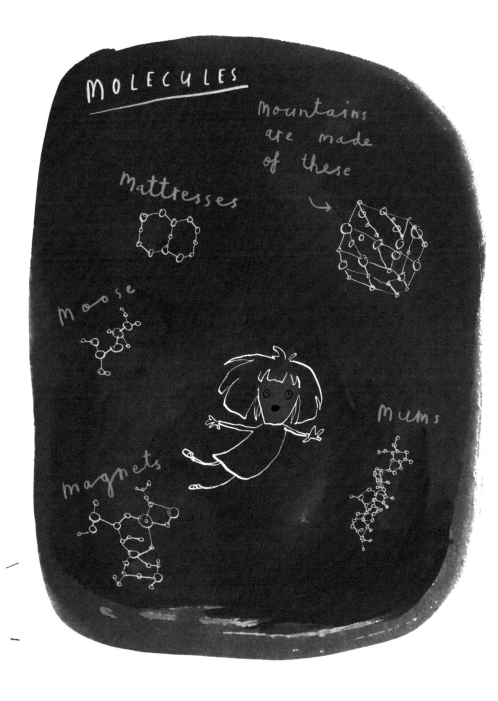

✗ Although matter makes
up all things, matter
itself is made of molecules

It's a minor miracle that they all
made it back out of the microscope
at their normal size again.

Nearly
NINE Thousand

The answer to the enigma* is:
nearly nine thousand. Sort of.

You could never actually fit
an elephant inside an envelope.

But you could fit nearly nine thousand
envelopes inside an elephant.

* See the letter E

Then again, it depends on the size
of the envelope, so never say never.

O o

ONWARD

Out on the ocean there
is an owl who rides on
the back of an octopus.

They search for problems.

They solve them.

They move on.

A Puzzled PARSNIP

Parsnips aren't known for their intelligence,
but this one was particularly daft.

Point proven.

Q q

The missing
Question

This story is supposed
to be about a question.

But I can't find it anywhere.

Do you know where it is?

R r

ROBOTS DON'T LIKE RAINClouds

Robots don't like rain clouds
So they steal them from the sky.

From everywhere and anywhere
That's why it's been so dry.

I'm sure you have been wondering,
What's with all this dust?

Well, robots don't like getting wet.
They don't do well with rust.

Sink or Swim

This is the story of a regular cucumber, who watched a programme about sea cucumbers and thought it might be a better life for him.

That very evening, the regular cucumber went to the shore and, taking a last look around, plunged into the sea.

However, never having tried before, he hadn't realised he couldn't swim, and sank straight to the bottom.

He hasn't been heard from since.

But don't worry...

...the owl and the
octopus are on their way!

The TERRIBLE TYPEWRITER

Tt

Not so long ago, and in a room not so far away, sat a typewriter and a terrified typist.

You see, whatever was written on this particular typewriter, however strange, had a terrible habit of coming true.

It was only a few moments before this typist's story...

...came to a tragic end.

It turns
out
the monster
has a taste
for typists
rather than
trees.

aw,
man!

UNDERGROUND

Unfortunately, Nigel wasn't
very good at climbing.

The other monkeys laughed
at him because he needed a
ladder to get up the tree.

This upset Nigel,
so he used his ladder
to move underground.

Turns out being underground
isn't so bad sometimes.

V v

VICTOR the VANQUISHED

Victor was used to being victorious.

But recently he was defeated and retreated into hiding under the stairs, where he now sits, plotting his vengeance.

One day they'll all be very sorry.

The WHIRAFFE

W w

The ingenious inventor had
a favourite invention of all –
the Whiraffe.

It had the head of a whisk
and the body of a giraffe.

They became great friends over
the years and enjoyed strawberries
and whipped cream.

The Whiraffe, of course,
whipped the cream.

The CASE of the MISSING X-RAY SPECTACLes

One terrible morning, Xavier woke to discover that his excellent pair of x-ray spectacles had been stolen.

He knew exactly who to call…

What the owl and the octopus
knew, that the burglar did not,
was that an extra pair existed.

A YETI, a YAK and a Yo-yo

A yeti up north
Bought a yo-yo of sorts
From a yak only yesterday.

But, here's the thing,

It didn't have string,

So this morning
He threw it away.

ZEPPELIN

Edmund the astronaut has made
some progress.

He purchased a Zeppelin and now drives
a steady four feet from the ground.

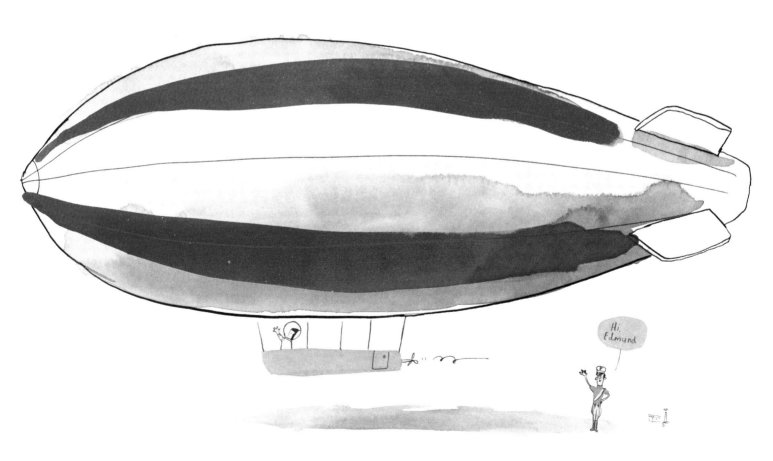

Only three hundred and twenty-eight
thousand, four hundred and twelve to go.